GAVIN

Trash Tastes Terrific

By Samuel Reynes

Edited by Tania Barlow

Illustrated by Dina Kalaitzi

A ISBN 9798649237376
B ISBN 9781716892424
eBook ISBN 9781716887246

For Gavin

1. I'M WHAT?

Yes, I may be a little overweight at the moment. Just a small, fat, round - but certainly cute - guinea pig. It is not my fault though. Who made hay so delicious? My owner says I can have an unlimited supply, so of course I am going to eat it all.

He is stingy with the veggies though. What I would do to have unlimited amounts of carrots and broccoli, spinach, lettuce and my absolute *favourite* – cucumber! It is just so juicy and green. I even like the loud munching sounds I make when I chomp down on a piece. But no, I only get one vegetable a day.

I would go outside but there are a few things stopping me. Firstly, we live in an apartment. I saw out the window once and we are incredibly high up. There is no way I would be able to make that jump.

Secondly, the metal cage I am kept in has me stuck at the side of the room on the floor.

My cosy cage is big enough for us. I do not live by myself, that would be horrible! No, I am incredibly lucky to live with my sister, Poppy and brother, Pepper. We get along simply fine. Obviously, we have our moments when we get on each other's nerves. Everyone can need their peace and quiet from time to time, and that is fine, we just need to respect each other's space.

Poppy can get excited sometimes. If she sees our owner moving in the mornings, she will instantly let out a high pitched wheek. We all *love* to wheek. We just cannot help it. If we get excited it happens. The feeling flows through our entire body and before we know it, we are shrieking our loud chirp for all to hear.

Pepper is the opposite. He never makes much of a sound, especially when the humans are around. But when they are not looking, he will push us out of the way of the food bowl and take the best bits for himself. He is older and stronger, so we struggle to take it back easily. He can outrun me too, being the athletic one. I would not be able to waddle quickly enough on my trotters.

'Poppy?' I ask, 'Why are we all different colours?'

Her face tells me she does not understand the question properly.

'Look. You have medium length white hair with caramel patches, Pepper over there has fairly short white hair with black patches and look at me!' I say, shaking my head rapidly and fluffing my coat. 'I look like I'm forever having a bad hair day. It's out of control, spiking out in every direction and I'm more of a charcoal and orange mix of colours!'

Poppy and Pepper, looking at each other, do not seem to know what to say. Pepper will not be any help, I bet he does not even know or care.

'Well, Gavin,' says Poppy. 'You see, we don't all have the same parents. We are all adopted. Owner Jim and his son, Owner Tommy adopted us. They came to my old house and took me and Pepper from our Mum when we were a few months old. After around six months they decided to add you, little pipsqueak, to our herd. I am not sure if they bought you from a pet shop or adopted you too. But that's why we're all different.'

I cannot believe this. I need to go and munch some hay and try to understand what Poppy just said. *Adopted?* I need more information.

'Poppy how can I be adopted? Owner Jim says he is my dad and Owner Tommy says he is my brother, and everyone says that us three are brothers and sisters. And I can't remember any other home.'

I can hear her sigh, but these are valid questions.

'Gavin, you don't have to be related by blood to be a brother or a sister. We are adopted into the same family and we're all guinea pigs so that does make us brothers and sisters. As for the Owners, I think that's just something they tell themselves so they feel a part of our herd. And you probably don't remember anything else from before because you were so small when you came into the home.'

'Interesting.'

And it is interesting. I always wondered why I had not grown up to be big and stand on two feet like the Owners, and why I was always so scared of them even though they are family. Something inside me just makes me run away. I just have so many things inside that I cannot control.

Oh no. Here is one now. I can feel my legs twitching. There is a wheek inside me, bubbling up to the surface. Imagine like when you feel a hiccup coming on, but the hiccup is filled with joy.

'Wheek!'

There it is, and now Poppy is joining in. We can hear it. Owner Tommy's footsteps coming towards our room. At this time of the morning, that means one thing. Vegetables are on their way. What will it be today? Oh, I cannot contain myself, I really hope we get cucumber. Please be cucumber.

'Pepper! I want it to be cucumber so bad!' I scream as he ignores me like usual.

The door handle is turning, and Owner Tommy enters the room. He has a small plastic blue bowl with him. That is where he hides the vegetables. I want to run to him and grab the snack, but I also want to run away because he is gigantic next to me. I am so torn. Owner Tommy is not the best balancer either; he might fall or stand on me.

I like to daydream about what is on the other side of the door. It only opens a crack every time and I can't see much. I like to imagine that there is a huge vegetable patch full of lettuce and of course, cucumbers which one day I will get to explore.

Standing on my back legs I still cannot see what is in the bowl. But my nose does not let me down. I have one keen nose. The fresh smell of juicy cucumber slices makes me perform another uncontrollable act. My owner loves to see me do this one although I am not sure why, I feel embarrassed by it.

When the excitement can't be dealt with by a wheek and boils over even more, I leap fully with all four hands and feet off the ground and spin around. Owner Jim says that I am 'Popcorning' because it is like a popcorn kernel popping around a pan as it heats up.

In all the excitement I did not notice that Owner Tommy was now holding his hand near my petal shaped ears. Normally I am very much on guard, but he has caught me by surprise. His index finger is only a few centimetres from my ear. I dart away under my chewed wooden house to safety.

Not this time Owner Tommy.

He got me a few times before. I will be honest it felt nice, but you can never be too careful. The Owners are so much bigger than us, and you must wonder why they adopted us. Maybe one day they will try and eat us. But not today, my podgy self managed to get away this time.

The smell of cucumber is very tempting though. Maybe I can edge out slowly. Just one foot in front of the other and keep low to the ground. My eyes are focussed on Owner

Tommy's hand holding a big piece of cucumber looking so fresh. If I will not claim it, for sure one of the others will.

As soon as I plant my two big front teeth into the soft cucumber surface, I can feel that Owner Tommy does not have the strongest hold of the piece. With a quick tug, I turn around victorious with the whole chunk as big as my head in my mouth. Giving off a quick squeal lets the other two know I am not sharing or to be disturbed as I enjoy my prize.

There is nothing better than cucumber. Nothing.

2. TOMMY

Owner Tommy, I say it all the time, is my favourite. I love the treats and even the heavy-handed strokes. He will learn to be gentler. He talks to me though, which is nice, but he is not able to understand what I say back. I try my best to let him know what I mean.

Picking me up from the cage, he is being quite gentle today. One hand keeping my front legs still, and the other on my bottom which makes me feel much safer. Sometimes he grabs in the cage with one hand and lifts me up, but that hurts me, so I nip him with my four front teeth. He seems to have learned that one quite quickly.

Either way, I do end up enjoying our adventure time, exploring the room. It is special too. It is some time away from the other guinea pigs and me and Owner Tommy

can play just the two of us. I am not
particularly good at playing. I get scared easily
and struggle to join in with his playtime games
like chasing a ball or anything like that. I
much prefer to hide, walk around exploring
and eat as much as possible.

We make our way over from the cage. I feel
like I am floating through the air, gliding
along high up in the sky. Owner Tommy takes
huge strides, much further than any of my
four little trotters could take me in one step.
Each of his would be the same as ten or more
of mine!

You get a really good view of the room from
up here. There is a fish tank with some
goldfish. They never talk to us though, and
there is a television, wardrobe, chair and a big
comfy looking bed. Four plump pillows and a
thick duvet spread across a bouncy mattress.
Owner Tommy puts me down and I can feel
the soft feathery quilt tickle my toes, my long
nails start to dig in like needles. Owner Jim
will be wanting to cut my nails again soon.
The worst time of the month.

Plodding around, there are new smells over
here. I can smell Owner Tommy much more

clearly. It is all so exciting that I start to wheek. I am trying to tell Owner Tommy 'Thank you for taking me out for playtime! I am really happy. This is a nice comfy quilt; it feels nice on my feet!' but it just comes out as noisy little squeaks that he is not able to understand.

'Aww do you like that, Gavin? Is that fun?' Owner Tommy says to me.

Maybe he can understand me. I shout another squeak at him to answer.

There is just one problem being out here though. There is nowhere to hide. I am scared that a bird or something will come and swoop down from above and take me away to eat me.

I start to look around to see anything I might be able to hide under. Owner Tommy reaches out to touch me, but I feel a little bit spooked, so I turn and run away. The big waves of quilt on the bed are hard to run through, especially with my big belly, so I must plod and jump my way across.

A dead end. As I reach the edge of the bed, there is nothing but a steep drop to the floor. A fall from up here would hurt me quite badly. That only adds to my fright and panic. I need to get down. I need to hide. I do not want this playtime anymore. Oh, why did we not have it on the floor like normal. There are vegetables when we do that and I can always run back into my cage or under the cupboard if I get like this, all scared.

I follow along the edge of the bed, looking for a way down. All the while, Owner Tommy is trying to grab me. Maybe *he* had decided to eat me.

Finally, there is an escape. A big pile of clothes at the side of the bed. I have heard Owner Jim tell Owner Tommy so many times to pick them up and put them in the wash, but he never listens. Now, it will be my saviour.

One leap of faith has me flying for real this time, without the safety of Owner Tommy's hands keeping me in place. I close my eyes so I cannot see how high from the ground I am.

The landing is soft, if a little smelly from all the dirty clothes. I pad around the surface but catch Owner Tommy making a move to grab me, so I burrow deep down, shuffling socks and underpants out of the way with my nose and tunnelling through t-shirts. It is nice, warm and dark in here.

The moving of clothes comes from above. Owner Tommy must be digging through to find me. He needs to be careful or he will throw me across the room.

A bright light comes from above. He has found me. With a full body jump, I leap out of the clothes pile and scan the room, spying the perfect hiding place under the bed. Owner Tommy plants one hand on my back but I manage to wriggle free and slide underneath the bedframe.

Owner Tommy shouts Owner Jim who comes running into the room.

'What have you done, Tommy?' Owner Jim asks angrily.

'Nothing dad, we were just playing, and he jumped off the bed and now he is hiding under it.'

'How many times have I told you not to take the guinea pigs on to the bed? What if they hurt themselves?'

'Sorry dad! I know. But help me! I can't reach Gavin.'

Both get on their knees and peer under the bed. They spot me quickly. The bed itself is a good hiding place from things coming from above, but not so good when the danger is on my level.

Owner Jim leaves while Owner Tommy tries to reach me with a broom handle and poke me out. I back up further and run away from the big plastic stick.

I hear the fridge door opening in the kitchen which sends me into a fit of loud wheeks because that sound almost always means vegetables will be coming soon.

Sure enough, Owner Jim enters and the smell of freshly cut vegetables runs up my nostrils. This is going to be hard to resist.

He kneels again, holding out my favourite juicy green vegetable. A succulent slice of cucumber. It is worth the risk, so I run full speed over to it. Owner Jim pulls it away a little from me just as I start to come out from under the bed. When I finally get my teeth into it, Owner Tommy scoops me up into the air again.

Before I know it, I am back in my cage again with Poppy and Pepper who are both chewing on some hay from the manger. I join them and say, 'Well, that was eventful.'

3. CLEANED OUT

The next morning, I hear heavy footsteps coming towards the room. Owner Jim is on his way, and he rarely brings snacks, especially if Owner Tommy has already fed us.

No, Owner Jim is usually coming to clean us out. He collects all our poop into a plastic bag, to do what with, I do not know - but I am not planning on using it so I guess he can have it. There is plenty more where that comes from but if he is getting paid for it, I certainly want a fair share for my efforts.

The door to the other side opens. That shining metal handle twisting. I can hear the spring inside tightening as Owner Jim presses it down.

'Hi Pigs,' he says just like every other time he comes in the door. We always respond the same way, with a small guinea pig grunt. No treats, no wheek, that is our rule. That is why

Tommy will always be our favourite. The treat giver.

There he is, standing so tall. Much bigger than Owner Tommy. Maybe three times as tall. He is wearing thick shoes that would squash me flat. He is equipped with his bright yellow rubber gloves, the fingertips still a little brown from yesterday's clean out. Normally there is a white plastic bag from a supermarket to collect our poop, but today he is holding a big black bin bag. It is already full of all sorts of interesting looking things and it smells terrific.

Trash is in there. Household trash. Leftover food from their dinner last night and breakfast this morning. I can even smell the cucumber ends that they rudely threw away without offering them to us.

I am going to sniff them out.

Owner Jim's knees click as he starts to kneel besides our cage. Me, Poppy and Pepper have all scampered to different corners and shelters. He might be trying to grab one of us after all. Every so often, one of us will be scooped up for one reason or another. The worst fear is that we could get taken to the vets. The last time I went there he poked and prodded all over. I hated it. Also, he never had any treats.

The cage door has been opened and Owner Jim is trying his best to shoo us with his hand out onto the floor. The tiles outside the cage are cold though so I am not a big fan of going out there very much. Maybe if they put a carpet down for us it would be better. Every time he reaches to shoo one of us, we all run in different directions to confuse him.

I give up. I want an easy life. I will just hop on out. I do like the sound my nails make clicking on the tiles. Plus, now I can get close to the big black bag. The smells are stronger now. Cucumber, obviously. There is also gravy, chips and lots of cardboard hidden inside.

Nothing is better for my teeth than chewing on a good bit of cardboard. I would rather that it had a little more flavour, but it's still fun to eat and play with.

This bag is heavy. There is a loud tumbling sound every time Owner Jim tosses a dustpan of poop into the bag.

A few nose nudges do not move it at all. I would chew through it, but the plastic bag does not look like it would taste nice.

Making a few attempts, I finally manage to hop up onto the rubbish bag. It makes a noisy rustle. I look over at Owner Jim who is too busy trying to scoop up the poop with one hand and stroke Poppy and Pepper with the other to notice.

'Messy pigs. Come here, Poppy. Do you like a scratch behind your ear?' he says.

He has a few beads of sweat trickling across his forehead from the task. He is pudgy like me and not great at anything that requires energy.

Climbing the side and peering in, I can see the wealth of treats and toys that would be going to waste.

I am going in.

GAVIN

4. CHUTE

It is unbearable trying to hold in the wheeks. What a fantastic place. How am I just finding out about diving in trash?

There is so much to rummage in. I am scared my nose will go bald from sniffing and nudging everything in the bag. It is dark though. Not much light can get in apart from through the big opening at the top.

I need to stay incredibly quiet; Owner Jim will shout at me for being in here for sure. This much fun should not be allowed.

Chewing on an empty cereal box, poop droppings fall all around me, giving me a fright until I realise what they are.

Still no sign of the cucumber ends. There are too many smells all at once inside so it is too hard to sniff in the right place.

The bag is starting to shake. There is no more poop coming in. I think Owner Jim has finished his collection.

'Okay, Pigs. All clean,' I can hear him say.

I should probably get out. He is going to notice he only has two guinea pigs any moment now.

But he does not. He has not noticed at all. I am a little bit angry that he does not see that I am not there. I am the important one, I am Gavin, the best guinea pig in the world. Pudgy and cute, everybody's favourite.

I slip on the cereal box and tumble further down the bag as I feel it being lifted into the air. I scurry up and into the box to hide, too scared to make a noise. My whiskers begin to tremble.

Rustling comes from above. Owner Jim is tying the top closed. I crawl out of my hiding place and try to find a way out of the bag. It is completely sealed and now pitch-black dark. I must rely on my sense of smell and my whiskers to see. The bag is too tough to poke my nose through.

Gnawing at the plastic, I realise I was right. It tastes terrible. It sticks in my mouth and is hard to spit out. It is working though. A small hole, enough to fit my small snout through, opens.

After pushing hard enough, my head emerges fully outside the bag. The floor moves by quickly underneath. I am high up; there is no way I could jump down at this height without hurting myself. Jumping is not going to work; I need another plan.

Come on, Gavin. You can do this. Where can I jump to? There is nothing around in the corridor. In truth it is a real disappointment that there is no vegetable patch here, that would make a soft and delicious landing right now.

I want to shout out to Owner Jim but he will be so angry with me and if I am an adopted member of the family, he might not think twice at giving me away to other people, and they might not have cucumber there, or any vegetables at all! I am not making that mistake and throwing this life I have away.

There is another door in front. It looks bigger and stronger than the one in the room. My stomach does a little flip as the bag drops to the ground.

Ouch.

A hard thud to the ground really hurts my back leg. I struggle to stand up, but this would be the best time to get out of the bag and run back to the room. All I want is to be back with my adopted brother and sister, munching on some hay. Fresh hay. How delicious. I already miss it. The crunch in the chew, the lovely yellow colour and the meadow smell. Fantastic.

Now I am hungry, I will have a snack on this box again. It is not the same and not nearly as good as my hay. It has no sort of strong tasty taste to it.

Come on, focus Gavin. I am letting myself get distracted. My belly will not be the boss of me today. I need to get out of this bin bag.

Nuzzling my head back out of the hole, I look around. Tommy! Tommy is over in the distance watching television in the living room. I will try to shout him over. Tommy is the good one, the one who brings me vegetables and gives me uncomfortable petting time. He would not be mad at me for getting in the bag, he will help me.

I squeak and wheek as loud as I can, but he can't hear me over the television. He is watching something loud with flashing lights. This is useless. I will just make a run for it. Run out of the bag and back to the door. Sit there until it opens and be back in my cage in no time.

Oh no! Owner Jim is trampling back towards me. His heavy shoes smashing into the floor and shaking everything around me. The shudder tickles my feet. He is scary though, so I run back and hide in my cereal box instead of getting squashed.

A few seconds go by before the bag is jolted back up into the air. This time I keep my balance a little better and made myself ready for the lift off. Some of the cans at the bottom of the bag crunch together under the weight of all the rubbish moving around.

I jut my head out of the small hole again. Owner Jim opens the big door, taking the rubbish bag out.

Goodbye home, goodbye Poppy and Pepper, goodbye Tommy. I am in real trouble now.

Now Owner Jim is reaching for a shiny metal handle on a shiny metal sheet on the wall. He pulls on it and it opens out like a big mouth. Inside is total darkness with noises of tumbling, falling items.

The bag raises up and sits wedged in the hole, shooting into the darkness after a few hard pushes from Owner Jim.

It feels like I am falling to the ground again. But the fall is taking a long time. The bag is falling faster and faster down the metal chute inside the building. Some of the items of trash inside the bag look weightless and start floating upwards.

A huge crash comes as I land with the bag on to what feels like a pile of other bags. Bracing for the crash this time, I manage to avoid getting too hurt, although my leg is still painful from before.

Be brave. I will have a look out and see where I have landed. What strange world I am in now.

Looking out, I can smell rotten vegetables and smelly stuff all around. My bag is sitting on top of a huge pile of other black bags.

A loud noise comes from above. Looking up, another rubbish bag is falling out of the bottom of the dark trash chute and lands on top of me and everything goes dark.

5. RATS

I wake up feeling fine, aside from a terrible headache pumping through my brain. After wriggling about I manage to clamber out of the rubbish mountain. I am close to the top, but it keeps growing every time another bag comes crashing down. Learning from my mistakes, I know to duck and hide when I hear the falling from the big dark hole above.

The rustling of black plastic is noisy underneath my feet. I step on a sharp object in one of the bags and let out a yelp! Looking down, one of my long nails is now short, being chopped off. It will grow back at least.

It is incredibly smelly down here and seems to be getting worse and worse. Still, there must be some good food around somewhere.

I start to nuzzle and rummage again, looking for the freshest thrown out vegetables. My nose is bouncing up and down, whiskers twitching, looking around for something tasty in the trash.

A half split open bag sits at the bottom of the trash mountain. My eyesight is not great, but I can almost smell something delicious. I am not sure whether it is broccoli or cauliflower as they both smell very much the same to me! As I get closer, I try to make out the colour; that will tell me for sure. One is green and the other is white.

Making my way down is a challenge, having to move left, right, going up to come back down just like following a hiking trail, only this one has not been trodden by feet over and over.

The colours become clearer, the vegetable is white cauliflower, almost fresh but with some of the ends becoming slightly brown. It will do though and should fill the space in my belly for a little while.

Just before I get to the biggest piece, something moves as quick as a flash in front of me, making my whiskers flutter in the breeze. The cauliflower was gone. Did the cauliflower see me coming? Are they alive out here in the wild and know when I am going to eat them? No, let us not be silly, Gavin. The cauliflower was old and going brown, it definitely did not know I was coming, plus I came from behind so it could not see me.

It does not matter. There are still a few more pieces lying around, that was just the biggest and best one. I will make do with a smaller chunk of cauliflower.

I bite down onto the trunk and can taste straight away that it was a little old. Also, it would have been much tastier if it had been a green broccoli. I can feel a tug at the other end of the cauliflower. Looking up there is a face a little bit like mine pulling the broccoli away.

I drop it, with the other face taking it all for themselves.

'Ah! What are you?' I shout, dropping any crumbs of cauliflower out of my mouth and onto the ground. Shaking, I say it again, 'What… who are y-you?'

They are much bigger than me in every way like how round they are and how tall and long too. They are dirty brown in colour with crooked bent whiskers and more pointy ears, not like my cute petal ones. Their faces seem sharper. And there is one *really* big difference. A big pink worm seems to be coming from their bottom!

The strangely familiar looking animal does not answer and turns and scurries away under a big metal rubbish bin on wheels.

The black bags keep falling and are now tumbling down the sides of the mountain like an avalanche. I make the decision to follow the creature into the safe looking hiding place.

As I enter slowly, I see around twenty beady eyes following me.

'Hello?' I ask. No response.

A pair of the eyes comes forwards and gets closer and closer to me. I can smell the creature, like it has been rolling in the bins for days, maybe even months, without giving itself a wash.

'Oi, who do you think you are?' says a frightening voice.

It seems to come from the eyes in front of me, so I respond in that direction, 'I - I'm G-G-Gavin the Guinea Pig.'

Silence fills the hiding place so much that I can almost feel it as a real thing in the air.

'Hahaha!'

Laughing now comes from every single one of the twenty eyes all around, echoing against the metal roof.

'A guinea pig? What is a pet rodent doing down here with the rats?' the main one said, still laughing.

'I fell from the sky. I got into one of those black bags and then fell down,' I say.

'Yeah, right,' the rat continued, 'Look everyone. This is Gavin, he's been thrown away by his owners because they don't love him anymore!'

They all burst out laughing at Gavin.

'That's not true!' I say, getting quite cross. 'My Owner Tommy and Owner Jimmy do love me. I just wanted to play in the bag, and they threw me out by accident. I am sure they will be missing me and looking for me right now!'

'I wouldn't get your hopes up, young Gavin. You see, a few pets find themselves down here every year, and they don't ever end up back with their owners. Mind, we don't get many other rodents, do we fellas? No, we usually get things like geckos, turtles, even the occasional kitten'.

The main rat comes closer to me.

'Let's go for a walk, Gavin,' he says.

We step out from the shelter and shadow of the big bin on wheels and into the barely lit garbage room.

A couple of smaller rats follow from behind.

'Why doesn't he have a tail, Richy?' one shouts in a squeaky voice.

The main rat turns, looks at my behind and then to the baby rat. 'He lost it in a fight,' he says and winks at me. 'Now go back inside.'

The little rat listens and scurries back under the bin, turning into just a pair of eyes again.

'The name's Richy. Richy Rat. It's nice to meet a guinea pig, truth be told. We're cousins you know.'

'Cousins?' I ask.

'Yeah, cousins. If you go back years and years, we have the same ancestors, but changed to be a bit different over time. Like our tails,' he said, holding up the pink worm.

'So that's what that is!' I say, 'Do you have to take it off to poop?'

Richy looks at me strangely so I change the subject.

'How many years? Like, ten?' I ask curiously.

'A little longer than that, Gav. We're talking millions.'

I do not quite believe him, neither that we are cousins nor that it happened millions of years ago. How can we be cousins if I do not even know his mum or dad? But I remember that family does not have to be by blood, so I go along with it. If Owner Tommy AND Poppy and Pepper can be my siblings, then this rat can probably be my cousin in this crazy world!

We start walking around the garbage room, along the bottom of the mountain of black bags.

'I'm telling you, Gav. We have got the life down here. All the free food you can eat. Most of it is pretty fresh. You would not believe the sorts of stuff people just chuck away,' Richy says.

'So, did you all get thrown away down the chute too?' I ask.

'Us? No mate. We moved here a few months back. Us rats are born on the streets, then go looking for a nice place to make a life for ourselves. Warmth, shelter and food - that's what we're after and it's all right here for us.'

'And the building doesn't mind you living here?' I say.

'Oh, no. The building, they don't like us,' Richy says, with his voice becoming nervous for the first time since I met him. 'They don't like us one bit. You stay out of their way. They try to squash us, trap us, poison us, you name it, they try it. We're just trying to get by you know.'

I do know. They do not seem like bad rodents. I am not sure why it is fine for me to live in the building, but they get chased away just because of where they were born or how they look.

'We come across a small stash of vegetables and cardboard, separated from the rest of the rubbish.

'Dig in my friend, you are our guest,' Richy Rat said.

I got so excited that a little wheek popped out. The look on Richy's face lets me know that this is not normal rat behaviour and I feel a little embarrassed.

'This tastes really good!' I say.

'Yeah, trash tastes terrific if you know where to look. There's an old saying, one man's trash is another rat's gold.'

Whilst I am in the middle of enjoying my dinner, a loud crunching noise comes from outside and a shrill beeping noise repeats over and over. The metal shutter door to the garbage room shoots upwards, letting the sunlight pour in and blind me for a moment.

Richy, startled, stands stiff on all four feet.

'It's the bin men, Gav.'

'What?'

'The bin men. Run!'

He turns, his tail brushing in front of my face and almost whipping me, then heads back to the bin. I follow.

The loud beeping stops as a large truck with a huge gaping mouth with metal teeth enters the garbage room. A huge roar from the engine rings all around and the smell of petrol pumps in. Two men in odd coloured outfits enter, stomping along in their big, heavy boots.

'Stay well clear of those boots, Gavin. They're specially made for squishing the likes of us,' Richy says in a whisper.

I nod, not wanting to make a peep. All I can see are the heavy boots crashing down on the ground all around the bin we are hiding under.

They start clearing the bin bag mountain piece by piece. I see the bag I came in on getting tossed into the truck's mouth and I feel a little sad that I never got to eat those cucumber ends.

Four big boots come to our sheltering bin. Two on each end and the wheels begin to move.

'Time to run again!' Shouts Richy Rat and all of us start darting in different directions to get away from the bin men in clunky boots.

Loud thuds sound out as the boots start stomping all around, trying to squish us.

'I'm a guinea pig!' I shout while running, but they cannot understand me, just like Owner Jim and Owner Tommy.

I take some shelter under a piece of a cardboard box and hear a thud and an 'Ouch' cry in a little voice.

'Got one,' said one of the bin men, laughing and scraping their shoe on the floor.

They tip the bin into the truck's mouth and then put it back where it was. The men get back into the front and drive away.

Once the shutter comes back down and the sunlight has been closed off again, Richy gives us the all clear.

'Everyone back under the bin. Is anyone hurt?'

Most of the rats stay quiet or say that they are fine. I am still panting trying to get my breath back.

'Oh no, look at little RoRo!' one cries.

The little baby rat from before crawls in slowly with a little bit of a funny walk.

'What happened?' asks Richy, concerned.

Little RoRo sobs a little and says 'They stomped on my tail. They got it; it fell off'. He looks at me and cheers up slightly. 'Now I'm just like Gavin!' he says in a happier voice.

It is dark but I can tell Richy is smiling.

'That was quite an ordeal. Happens more than we would like, too. Look Gavin, you stay here tonight, those bin men won't be back again for a while now. Get some rest and we can plan to get you out of here and back upstairs tomorrow,' Richy says.

I do feel tired, so agree and find a nice corner by the wheel to rest.

6. HOME TIME

I had a good night's sleep if truth be told. There was no real noise throughout the night, and it was much warmer than I had expected. Even the trash chute quietened down overnight.

I sit quietly and wait patiently for the rest of the rat herd to wake up.

'Right then, breakfast time everyone,' Richy says to the whole group.

'But what about getting me back upstairs?' I say a little impatiently.

'We'll get to that, Gavin mate. But first, breakfast. It's the most important meal of the day my old mum used to say.'

Despite the grumble going on in my belly - I may even have lost weight with all the running yesterday too - I decide to stay put and wait for them to finish their breakfast.

When they finally return, I greet them with an impatient tapping foot, letting them know that I am ready to go home now.

'Alright Gav, follow me,' Richy says.

We slip through a rusted off corner of the metal shutter and the wind hits my face. The sunshine feels nice on my hair and I feel instantly uplifted.

'Keep close to the wall, you don't want anyone to see you,' Richy tells me.

'Why not?' I ask, 'People love guinea pigs.'

'You don't look like a guinea pig right now mate. You have bin juice matting your hair, dirt all over you and you smell just like us. You could pass for RoRo the tailless rat right now. They're not going to stop and inspect you. If you scurry past, they'll see you as a rat and stomp you.'

Taking a few steps forward I say, 'So how do we get in? Can I climb?'

I scratch at the wall with my foot which is missing a nail. I try to plant all four feet and start to climb up, but it makes a sharp scratch sound and I just slide right back down.

'No. Too smooth and steep for me to climb. How about the front door?'

'You can't just walk in the front door, Gavin'.

'Yes, I can. Watch me.'

I make my way across the brick path and hop up onto the step of the building, dodging and swerving the feet of people passing by, without them noticing me.

Two big glass doors stand in front of me. I look back and Richy is just watching me from a distance. I move forward and the doors do not see me and do not open. I move forward again. This time, the doors slide open and a blast of cool air conditioning wind flows through my fluffy hair. It was not opening for me though. It opens for the security guard who is coming storming out with a straw broom held above his head.

'Hello, I live here, I just need to get back inside to…'

Thwack.

The broom comes crashing down beside me. I jump, turn and scamper back to Richy. I am out of breath from the short run.

'Told you it wouldn't work,' he says in a smug voice. 'I'll be honest, I've never really tried to get into the building past the garbage room - why would you want to? - so I'm not sure I'll be much help mate.'

I think as hard as I can.

'Wait. I have heard Owner Tommy talk about something before. Some spider that was trying to climb. It went… it went. I can't remember what it climbed.'

I search my brain again.

'A waterspout! The spider climbed up a
waterspout. I will do that. What's a
waterspout?' I ask.

'I don't know, Gavin. Is it like a drainpipe?
You're probably just about small enough to
squeeze into one of those, but you're not a
spider. I think they are better climbers than us
rodents,' Richy says.

'Let's try it,' I say as I run straight past the
front door and down the side of the building.

'Here, this black pipe with water trickling out
of it. This must be the waterspout!'

'Give it a go then, mate.'

So, I do. I fit my big round bottom into the
pipe and start walking along inside. The walls
are slippery, and I feel like I am on ice skates
trying to keep my balance.

A surging roar comes at me down the pipe. It
gets closer and closer until I see a flood of
water bubbling down towards me. The water
sweeps me off my feet and pushes me all the
way back out of the pipe, spinning round as I
end up on my back in front of Richy.

'Oh yeah,' I remember. 'The same thing happened to the spider too.'

Richy looks at me and sees I am running out of ideas. He seems to begin thinking hard.

During the lull, I look around for inspiration. I notice lots of small black boxes dotted around. They are plastic with a circular hole in each end, similar in size to the pipe I was just in.

'Hey Richy, what are those black boxes all around?'

He stares at me and I feel as though I asked a bad question; it seemed to hit him hard.

'Don't ever go in there,' he said sternly. 'It is apparently filled with the tastiest, finest food you could ever wish for. But any rodent that ever went in, has never come out again. Promise you will never go in the black box, no matter how tempting it smells. Stay out of there. Promise me, Gav.'

'Sure, I promise,' I say whilst thinking about what delights would be awaiting inside there. I bet it is cucumber. There is simply nothing better I can think of.

'There is another way,' Richy says, focusing on his thoughts. 'At the back of the building, near the not-so-good bins which have mostly rotten food and where the alley cats like to hang out, there is an air vent. That will lead you inside, but I don't know where to exactly.'

'Great, we will try that,' I say, getting up onto my feet again and shaking off the water like a dog.

7. MAZE

'Stay close, you don't want to get picked off by the cats,' Richy tells me, making me worried.

I can hear the growls and meows in the distance, lurking around the bins. I am not able to see any cats though. I am not sure if I feel relieved or more worried that they are hiding, ready to pounce.

'Quickly, keep up,' Richy orders as I move my feet to carry my fat body, trying to do it at the same speed as him. This is hardly fair; he has had lots of practice of living in the wild and running around. Plus no one is bringing him snacks to fatten up on all day long. This has been a wakeup call though. Once I am back in that room, I will be on a strict diet to get in better shape.

The sky is a lovely blue colour with no clouds in sight. This is the first time I have ever been outside. Obviously, I have seen it out of the window, but this is completely different. The smells, the breeze, the warmth from the dazzlingly bright sun. You cannot experience all this from inside, behind a glass sheet. I wonder what rain feels like.

I feel my hair, still damp, and assume it would be similar. I am starting to smell like a wet dog after a jump in a river. I am almost literally a drowned rat, something Owner Jim says when he comes home and it has been raining. He does want to feel close to me and my cousins, surely.

'You see it, Gav? Right up there. You'll need to jump on those boxes, make your way across to the big metal bin, try not to fall in, jump up onto the air vent ledge and push yourself through the bars. Easy,' Richy says.

I do not think it is easy though. Easy for him to plan, and it might look easy, but doing it will not be. I am not a gymnastic guinea pig, but a stumpy little fat potato. What will probably happen is I will jump up and fall straight through the boxes and come crashing back down. Everyone, even the hungry alley cats, will probably come along just to laugh at me. Gavin the chunky guinea pig falling flat on his face.

I want to go home. I miss the Owners and I miss Poppy and Pepper. I will do it. For them. They must be miserable without me in their life! Plus, I really could do with having a bath sometime soon.

'Right. I'll give it a try then,' I say, unsure of how it is going to turn out.

I prepare myself mentally and inspect the obstacle course before me. Now the boxes look mouldy, too. They might just crumple in on themselves at the slightest touch.

'I can do it,' I tell myself.

Richy looks around. I know he is nervous inside and keeping an eye out for predators. It is not just me who is scared.

'Here. I. Go.'

I run at full speed, my feet making a clapping noise they are moving so fast. I have not gone at this sort of speed since I was a young pup getting 'the zoomies' and uncontrollably running round my cage in circles.

Just at the right point, I leap up into the air. My back arches as the weight of my belly pulls me towards the ground. My front feet catch the edge of the cardboard box and the others continue to pedal as fast as they can to fling me up on top of the box.

This looks like quite a tasty box.

'Not now Gavin,' I say out loud.

I breathe heavily, trying to catch as much air as possible into my lungs. From where Richy is standing, I must look like a balloon inflating and deflating repeatedly.

The next bit is to get from here and across the boxes without them collapsing. The edges feel stronger, so I stick to them and go around. The rim of the bin looked close to the boxes from the ground, but now I am up here there

is a gap with a big drop all the way back down
to the ground.

The run-up worked before, so I try it again. I
back up as far as I think the box will hold my
weight during take-off. I run again, this time a
little slower as my energy is down. I make it
into the air and fly towards the edge of the
bin. I remember what Richy told me. 'Try not
to fall in'. I can see why; the ledge is very thin.
The landing will have to be perfect to not slip
in.

All four legs land and cling on to the bin's
rim. I am perched like a budgie in a cage,
swinging a little as I try to shift my weight and
stay balanced.

One last challenge before I am inside the
building. The bars on the air vent. Again, they
looked much wider before. It will take so
much effort to squidge myself through there.

My whiskers prickle on the cold bars and
smush backwards. They are telling me I am
not going to fit through here. I need to prove
them wrong.

My head pokes through without a problem. So does my neck. Shoulders are a squeeze, but I slip in one foot at a time. Now for the challenge. My big round belly. I drag myself forward with my front feet and push with all my strength with my back feet. I could really use a snack right about now.

I can feel the inside of my belly sloshing around as the bars squeeze hard against my sides. Eventually, I shoot through and roll over, headfirst, and make a bang as I land on my bottom hard against the freezing cold metal vent.

It is a maze in here. I try to use my nose to sniff out where my house might be, but it is too cold. No smell seems to be coming through.

I do know I live on a higher floor though. The building is fifteen floors high. I don't live at the top but definitely above halfway. I make my way up the air vent system going higher and higher until I feel I have covered the right amount of distance.

Still no smells becoming clear, I decide to tip tap through and investigate different apartments and see if I can spot mine.

The first home I look into has an angry dog who smells me coming and starts barking crazily at the air vent in the top corner of his room. I quickly run away and check others.

I have been in the air vent for a while now. The cold is starting to bite at my nose and my toes. There are loud sounds coming from all the different apartments with barking dogs, loud televisions and crying. Wait, I know that crying. It belongs to Owner Tommy. He sounds the same as when Owner Heather stopped coming home. She was coughing a lot and stopped coming in the room to see us much and then she stopped coming all together. That was when Owner Tommy made this crying sound for days and days.

Running excitedly to the vent where the crying is coming from, I can start to smell the familiar scents of my home. Poppy and Pepper have been pooping a lot recently, I can smell it.

I reach the air vent grid that is above the cupboard in Owner Tommy's room. I cannot fit through this grid. It does not have long bars, instead it is in a pattern of small squares not big enough to fit my littlest toe through.

I can see Poppy and Pepper plodding around their cage whilst Owner Tommy sobs on his bed. Excited to see everyone again, I let out a big wheek.

The two guinea pigs are looking around for me, but Owner Tommy did not hear. I build all my remaining energy and put it into a string of some of the loudest wheeks I have ever done in my life.

Owner Tommy wipes his face dry of tears and looks up. Suddenly he does not seem sad anymore.

'Dad. Dad! He's back. Gavin. He's back!'

Owner Tommy is as happy to see me as much as I am to see him.

Owner Jim comes rushing in and looks around the room.

'What, where?' he says.

That is nice. Owner Jim does not let me know he likes me that much very often, but I can see in his face he is relieved that I am back and safe.

'He's up there, dad. In the air conditioning vent,' Owner Tommy says.

'How on Earth did he get up there? Have you been messing about with it?' Owner Jim replies.

'No! I don't know how he got up there. Quick! Get him down before he runs off.'

8. STUCK

Owner Jim runs off, almost stepping on the cage housing Poppy and Pepper. They have finally noticed that their favourite adopted brother is home. Both have their front feet up against the wires of their cage wheeking. Even Pepper cares!

They tire themselves out quickly with the excitement and must stop for a snack break and chew on some hay. I cannot wait to get down there and munch on some myself. Nice clean food.

Owner Jim comes back holding a toolbox and a step ladder.

'Out the way Tommy,' he says while folding out the ladders.

He climbs up and I can see his face in line with mine. We have never been at the same height before. I feel important, and close to him.

Owner Jim pulls out a screwdriver and starts to unscrew the grid from the wall. It comes off and dust falls in his face, making him sneeze.

He reaches in and tries to grab me, but I dodge him and run out of the way. I try to tell him that I cannot help it, it is just my instincts and I can't control them, but it just comes out as little scared squeaks that he thinks means I'm scared and stupid.

I run to the edge of the vent now the grid is no longer there. It is incredibly high up. I have never been so high up, ever.

Wind is blowing my hair forward and covering my eyes. I can see the pile of clothes still there - Owner Jim will not be happy about that - but it is too high to jump into safely this time. The bed is just out of my jumping reach too.

'Don't jump, just trust them,' shouts Poppy. My sister always looks out for me.

'I've got an idea!' says Owner Tommy as he runs out of the room. Poppy and Pepper dart into their hiding houses, knowing the clumsy boy might well topple onto them.

He comes back holding the sweetest smelling thing ever. A tasty, juicy, fresh, lime green, massive piece of cucumber.

I will do literally *anything* for a good slice of cucumber. My favourite person has delivered once again. I close my eyes and leap with all my faith and let out a giant wheek. I can feel my hair ruffle in the wind as I fall and the sound of myself dropping through the air. The sound of my wheek still echoing around the room.

My eyes open with a jump as I land safely in Owner Jim's hands. He caught me just before I could get to the cucumber. Luckily, Owner Tommy holds it out and I start to nibble at it. That is why he's my favourite.

Owner Jim gives my hair a tussle and plants a wet kiss on top of my head. It is really embarrassing in front of my siblings.

'We've missed you little man. We were worried,' he says, and I try to smile back at him. He passes me over into the arms of Owner Tommy who cuddles me with his face. I gently lick his cheek to say that I am glad to be home. It is salty from his tears.

'I'm so glad you're okay, Gavin,' he says, as happy tears start falling down his face.

They place me back in my cage and I shake to fluff up and fix my hair.

GAVIN

9. FAMILY

'You stink!' Poppy yells at me, 'Give yourself a wash right now.'

I start to nibble at my hair and try to clean it but there is too much mess. Plus, it tastes awful.

'Where on Earth have you been, Gavin?' she asks.

'Oh, were you gone?' says Pepper, pretending not to be interested again.

'Guys it was incredible!' I say, 'I mean, it was really scary to be honest but the adventure of a lifetime. I thought getting lost in a pile of clothes was eventful yesterday, but this was so much more. I went down the trash chute and had to find my way back up. I met Richy and the rest of our cousins down there...'

'Who is Richy?' says Poppy.

'Oh, Richard the Rat is his full name, but he likes to be called Richy. I saw him and little RoRo Rat. All our cousins.'

I notice Poppy and Pepper give each other that look again when they try to pass information without saying anything. This time they seem more confused than anything.

'Rats?' Pepper says, suddenly more interested.

'Gavin, rats are not our family,' says Poppy.

'Yes, they are. They said they are our cousins. We go back millions of years but are just a little different,' I protest.

'They are not family,' Pepper snaps.

It goes quiet and a little awkward between us all. 'But you don't have to be blood relatives to be family,' I say.

They both laugh and realise how right I am, 'Well we'll have to meet these cousins sometime,' says Poppy.

We hear a rustling noise coming from above along with a small, quiet squeak.

'There they are!' I say. 'It's Richy, RoRo and everyone else.'

'We followed you up here. Just wanted to make sure you got back safely,' says Richy, 'It's a nice little setup you have here.'

All three of us are so excited to see them, we start wheeking and popping and bouncing around our cage, even Pepper.

Owner Jim is climbing his ladder to put the grid back on the air vent when he is met by ten rats in front of his face.

'Ah! What are these rats doing here? Tommy, quick. Get the spray!' he shouts. He looks back at the rats, screams and falls backwards off his ladder.

'You best get out of here,' I tell them, 'that spray will not be nice for you. We'll come down and see you in the garbage room soon though, I promise.'

'Please do!' squeaks RoRo and they turn and scamper back down the vent.

Owner Jim is still catching his breath as Owner Tommy rushes in with a red can in his hand. Ignoring it, I turn to Poppy and Pepper.

'I'll take you to see them, but we need to find an easier way down than the chute!'

We all gather round the hay manger and snack quietly whilst thinking of the fun we'll have with our cousins in the future.

Owner Jim fixes the grate back on to the wall and checks that there are no more rats running around. He comes over to us and all that can be heard is the three of us chomping on the strands of hay. Owner Jim and Owner Tommy come down to our level and reach in, giving us all a stroke and scratch behind the ears. This is a great life. My family, adopted or not, my food and my home. I would not leave this behind for the world.

GAVIN

GAVIN

ABOUT THE AUTHOR

Samuel Reynes is a new children's author. Working in the education sector has given a unique understanding and aided in writing for the specific audience. Influences have come from being raised in the North of England followed by a professional career in the Middle East, offering an insight into a range of cultures.

If you like this book, a review on any online platform would be most welcome. For more information and books, head over to the website www.samuelreynes.com

Printed in Great Britain
by Amazon

56001272R00050